This book belongs to:

MeJan

Contents

Cover illustration by Colin King
Illustrations on pages 32-33 by Peter Stevenson

Published by Ladybird Books Ltd
80 Strand London WC2R ORL
A Penguin Company
15 17 19 20 18 16 14
© LADYBIRD BOOKS LTD MCMXCVII, MMI
LADYBIRD and the device of a Ladybird are trademarks of Ladybird Books Ltd

Printed in China

Off to school

written by Catriona Macgregor
illustrated by Colin King

My chair,

my table,

my book,

my painting,

my teacher,

my class,

my school!

Just pretending

written by Catriona Macgregor
illustrated by David Pattison

I am an astronaut.

I am a doctor.

I am a lion.

I am a dancer.

I am a monster.

I am a diver.

I am me!

The school play

written by Catriona Macgregor

illustrated by David Pace

This is the prince.

This is the princess.

This is the horse.

This is the dragon.

This is the giant.

This is the fairy.

This is the school play!

In the house

written by Shirley Jackson

illustrated by Valeria Petrone

A boy and a book,

a mum and a mouse,

a dad and a dog,

a girl and a house.

New words introduced in this book

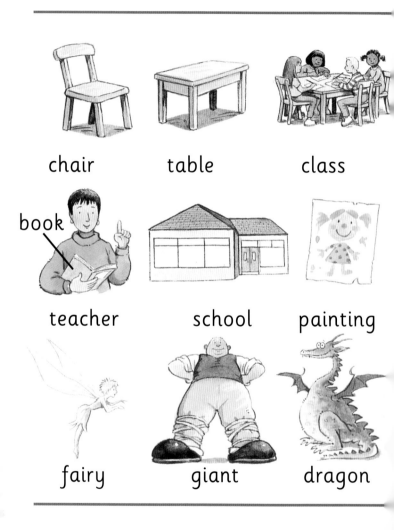

chair   table   class

book

teacher   school   painting

fairy   giant   dragon

am, an, and, I, me, play

The school play

First look at the pictures and talk about what is
happening. Why are the children dressed up? What is
the play about? Has your child ever seen a play?
Were there any funny or sad parts she can remember?
Now read the story to your child, pointing to the words
at the bottom. Then read it with her before encouraging
her to read it by herself.

In the house

Your child has already met many of the words in this
rhyme and may want to try to read it to you first.
Encourage her to look at the pictures for help.

New words

Look at these words with your child.
Can she use the pictures to help her
to remember what some of the
words say? Can she look through
the stories and find some of the
words again? (Vocabulary used
in the titles of the stories
is not listed.)

Read with Ladybird

Read with Ladybird has been written to help you to help your child:

- to take the first steps in reading
- to improve early reading progress
- to gain confidence

Main Features

- **Several stories and rhymes in each book**

This means that there is not too much for you and your child to read in one go.

- **Rhyme and rhythm**

Read with Ladybird uses rhymes or stories with a rhythm to help your child to predict and memorise new words.

- **Gradual introduction and repetition of key words**

Read with Ladybird introduces and repeats the 100 most frequently used words in the English language.

- **Compatible with school reading schemes**

The key words that your child will learn are compatible with the word lists that are used in schools. This means that you can be confident that practising at home will support work done at school.

- **Information pullout**

Use this pullout to understand more about how you can use each story to help your child to learn to read.

But the most important feature of **Read with Ladybird** is for you and your child to have fun sharing the stories and rhymes with each other.